ENDORSEMENTS FOR THE JESUS MOMENTS SERIES

"Jesus is always far better and far more interesting than we think he is, and seeing how the Old Testament points to him is a great way to find out how. These wonderful books will help us see more and more of Jesus."
SAM ALLBERRY, Associate Pastor at Immanuel Church, Nashville;
Author of *Why Bother with Church?* and *James For You*

"When we teach children that the stories from the Old Testament culminate in Christ, they begin to understand that he is the center of the Bible's story. This series highlights Jesus, the hero of every Bible story, and encourages readers to keep him at the center of their stories too."
HUNTER BELESS, Founder and Host of the Journeywomen podcast;
Author of *Read It, See It, Say It, Sing It*

"I smiled from ear to ear. My daughters came alive when they caught on. Hidden in this engaging true story is another *even more exciting*. We flipped backward and forward, all the while learning the biblical story and freshly encountering Christ."
DAVID MATHIS, Senior Teacher and Executive Editor at desiringGod.org;
Pastor of Cities Church, Saint Paul; Author of *Rich Wounds*

"We want our kids to see that the Old Testament points to Christ. In her marvelous *Jesus Moments* series, Alison Mitchell helps children seek and find the Old Testament connections to Jesus in fun ways they'll be sure to remember!"
DANIKA COOLEY, Author of *Bible Investigators: Creation; Bible Road Trip*™
and *Help Your Kids Learn and Love the Bible*

"Alison Mitchell draws children into a rich, true way of reading the Old Testament. The books are fresh, lively, attractive, intriguing and thought-provoking. Warmly recommended."
CHRISTOPHER ASH, Author and Writer-in-Residence at Tyndale House, Cambridge

"This *Jesus Moments* series is a delight! The clear and plain teaching of God's word, coupled with the intriguing illustrations and cleverly hidden symbols, make these books a win-win!"
MARY K. MOHLER, President's wife at SBTS in Louisville, Kentucky; Founder and Director of Seminary Wives Institute; Author of *Growing in Gratitude*

"What a clever series! By using symbols that children must find and explore, these books draw out significant links between Old Testament characters and Jesus. Perfect for parents and teachers who want to help their children understand God's big story."
BOB HARTMAN, Author of *The Prisoners, the Earthquake, and the Midnight Song*
and YouVersion's *Bible App for Kids*

Jesus Moments: Esther
© The Good Book Company 2025

Illustrated by Noah Warnes | Design & Art Direction by André Parker | All rights asserted

"The Good Book For Children" is an imprint of The Good Book Company Ltd
North America: thegoodbook.com UK: thegoodbook.co.uk Australia: thegoodbook.com.au
New Zealand: thegoodbook.co.nz India: thegoodbook.co.in

ISBN: 9781802541281 | JOB-007977 | Printed in India

Jesus Moments
Esther

Finding Jesus in the story of Esther

Written by **Alison Mitchell**   Illustrated by **Noah Warnes**

Did you know that the oldest stories in the Bible are a bit like puzzles? If you look carefully, you can spot some

"Jesus moments".

These are moments when someone or something in the story is a little bit like **Jesus**.

So this book is the exciting true story of how God used **Queen Esther** to rescue his people. But what makes it even more exciting is that it's also about **Jesus,** the greatest Rescuer of all.

As you read about **Queen Esther**, keep a lookout for some hidden **scrolls**. Each time you spot one, that's a clue that there's a **Jesus moment** to find as well.

So let's get started...

Haman was Number Two in the land of Persia. Only the king was more important.

And the king had said that everyone had to bow before Haman.

But one man — a Jew called Mordecai — refused. He would not bow, because he knew that Haman hated the Jews. This, of course, made Haman hate the Jews even more.

"I hate them so much," thought Haman. "In fact, I hate them so much that I want to get rid of them all."

And so he hatched a wicked plot...

Haman whispered to the king, "There are people in your kingdom who don't obey you. Make a law against them and I will get rid of them for you."

The king listened to Haman and made a very bad law. A law that no one could break — not even the king. Now the Jews were in desperate trouble.

But the king didn't know — and neither did Haman — that Esther, the queen, was Jewish.

Esther and Mordecai were from the same family. In fact, Mordecai had adopted Esther and brought her up to love and serve God.

So, when Mordecai heard about the very bad law, he told Esther, "You must go to the king and beg him to save our people".

But nobody could just go and talk to the king. No one at all – not even his queen.

If the king wasn't pleased to see Esther, she would be killed! (This was another very bad law.)

Esther was very, very scared.
What would she do?

"I know it's dangerous," said Mordecai. "But maybe you have become queen of Persia for such a time as this."

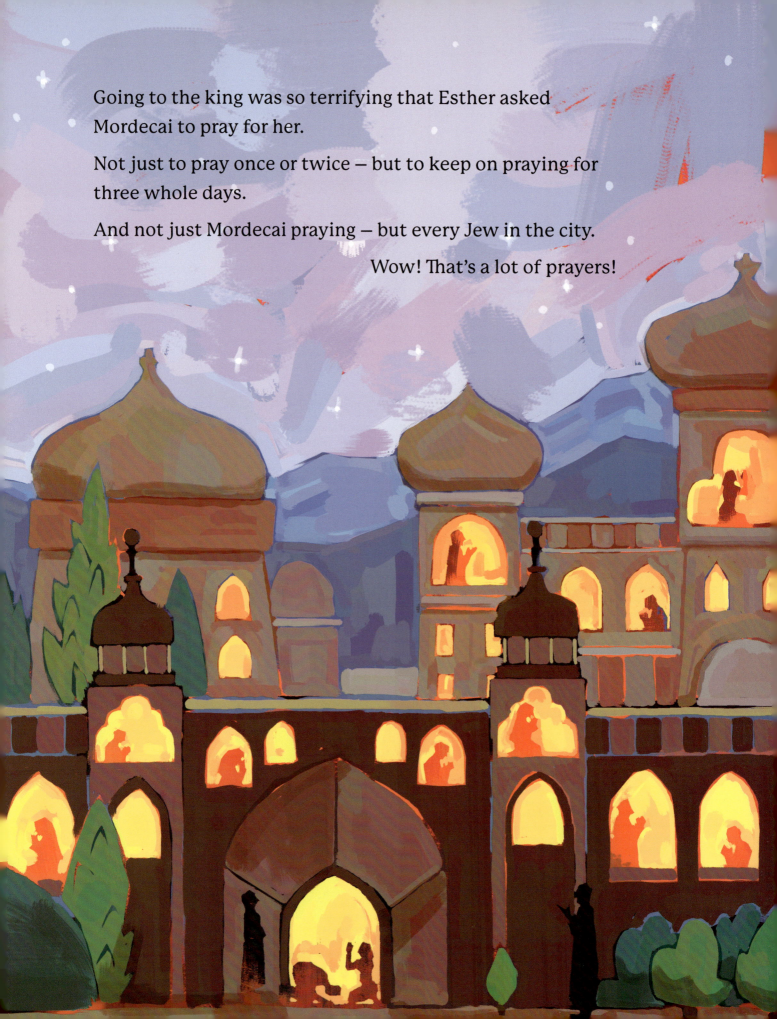

Going to the king was so terrifying that Esther asked Mordecai to pray for her.

Not just to pray once or twice — but to keep on praying for three whole days.

And not just Mordecai praying — but every Jew in the city.

Wow! That's a lot of prayers!

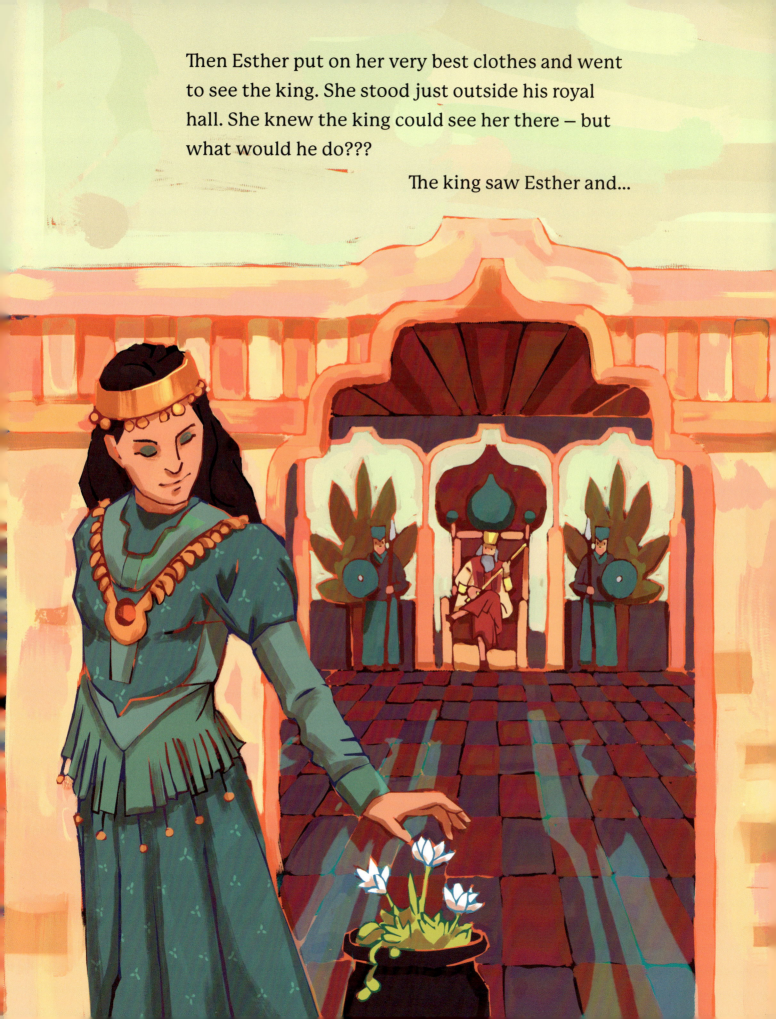

... he was very happy!

He held out his golden sceptre to show that she could come up to his throne. "What can I do for you?" he asked. "You can even have half my kingdom!"

"Please come to a special banquet with me," she said. "And bring Haman too."

The banquet was delicious. So the king and Haman were delighted when Esther asked them to come to another one the next day.

But that night the king couldn't sleep. He tossed and turned; he counted sheep; but nothing worked. So, he asked for the king's book of history to be read to him.

His servant read to him about the time when someone had rescued the king from a plot against him. And that someone, the book said, was… Mordecai!*

*You can read this story in Esther 2 v 21-23

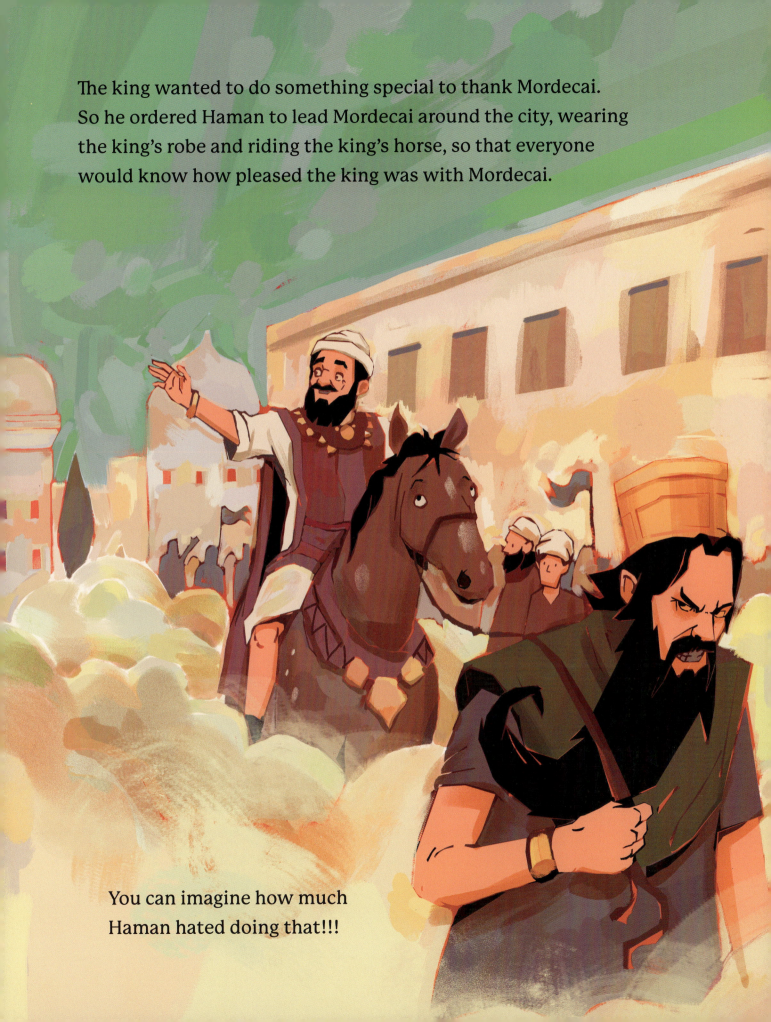

The king wanted to do something special to thank Mordecai. So he ordered Haman to lead Mordecai around the city, wearing the king's robe and riding the king's horse, so that everyone would know how pleased the king was with Mordecai.

You can imagine how much Haman hated doing that!!!

Now it was time for Esther's second banquet.

But at that banquet, Esther looked very sad.
"What is wrong?" the king asked. "How can I help you?"

"An enemy has set a wicked plot to kill me and my people," she said. "Please save us."

"What??! Why??! Who did this??!!!" shouted the king.

"It was Haman," she replied. "He is my enemy."

Then the king was so angry that he had Haman taken away and killed.

Hooray!!! The enemy had gone. The plot had failed. Or had it...?

Do you remember the very bad law the king made? The one that nobody, not even the king, could break? That law still said that all of the Jews would be killed.

But now the king made a new law. He told the Jews that they could protect themselves from their enemies. And that's what they did.

From then on, for hundreds of years, God's people enjoyed an annual festival called Purim, when they celebrated being saved from their enemies.

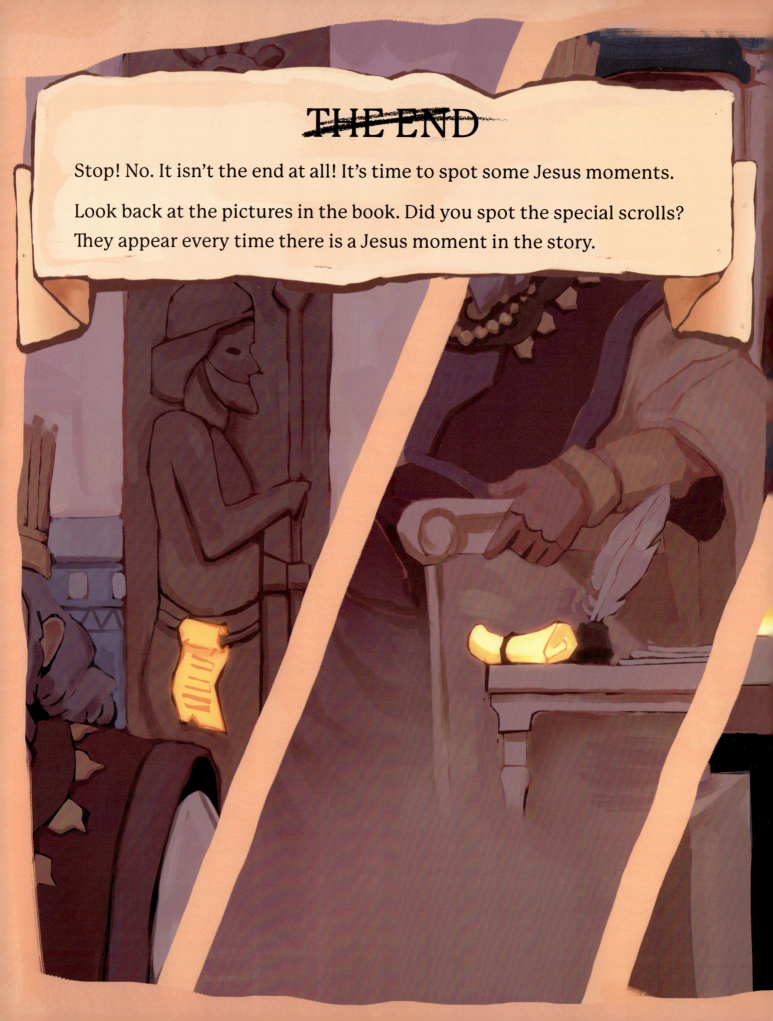

~~THE END~~

Stop! No. It isn't the end at all! It's time to spot some Jesus moments.

Look back at the pictures in the book. Did you spot the special scrolls? They appear every time there is a Jesus moment in the story.

Each Jesus moment is a moment when something in the story of Esther shows us a little bit about Jesus, the Son of God. Did you find them all? Here's what they mean...

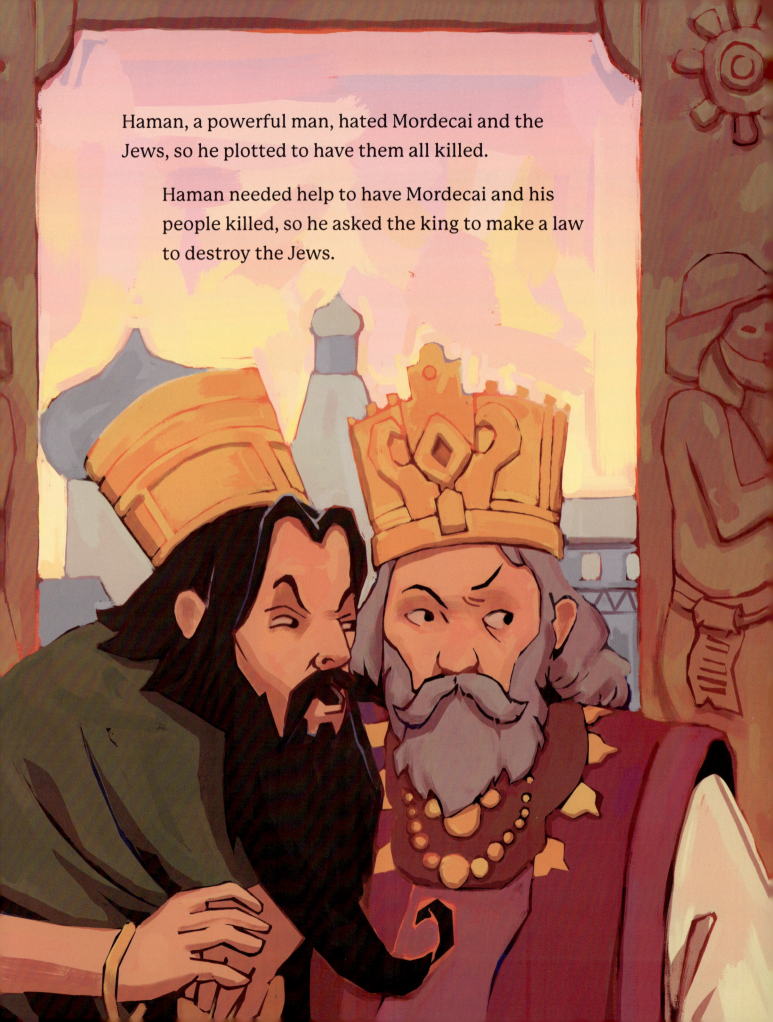

Haman, a powerful man, hated Mordecai and the Jews, so he plotted to have them all killed.

Haman needed help to have Mordecai and his people killed, so he asked the king to make a law to destroy the Jews.

At the time of Jesus, the powerful religious leaders hated him, so they plotted to have Jesus killed as well.

The religious leaders needed help to have Jesus killed, so they asked the Roman governor, Pilate, to have Jesus crucified.

Esther risked her life to beg for her people to be saved. She became queen of Persia for "such a time as this" (Esther 4 v 14).

Jesus was God the Son. He became a human being at just the right time so that he could give his life to save everyone who trusts in him.

The king's very bad law could not be ignored or ended, not even by the king himself.

God's very good law against sin cannot be ignored either. The price for our sin, our rebellion against God, had to be paid — and it was paid by Jesus when he died on the cross for us.

An annual festival, Purim, was set up to celebrate God's people being rescued from their enemies.

Christians today enjoy festivals every year to celebrate Jesus — especially Christmas and Easter.

Christians also meet every Sunday, when we remember how Jesus died to rescue God's people from their sin — and how he came back to life again to show that God really will save everyone who trusts in Jesus.

That's a great reason to celebrate!

Why look for "Jesus Moments"?

The oldest parts of the Bible were written hundreds or even thousands of years before Jesus was born, and yet they all point to him! And when we read the accounts of many Old Testament characters, we can see moments when they are a little bit like Jesus himself.

These "Jesus Moments" help us to see Old Testament stories afresh and to understand more deeply who Jesus is and why he came.

The Old Testament book of Esther tells us how God chose this young woman to become queen of Persia. We can see God's hand at work at every stage, from Mordecai stopping the plot against the king to Esther spending a year in beauty school before being chosen out of many other women. We have only touched on a few parts of her life in this storybook. If you read the full Bible account, you will spot other "moments" when something in the life of Esther pointed towards the life of Jesus Christ, the Son of God.

It was always God's good plan to send his Son to live on Earth, to die for our sins and then to rise to life again. And God gave his people lots of clues about how this would happen.

The risen Jesus told his followers that the Old Testament Scriptures are about him: "And beginning with Moses and all the Prophets, he explained to them what was said in all the Scriptures concerning himself" (Luke 24 v 27). So when we read exciting Old Testament stories, we can look out for those same clues — those "Jesus moments" that point to the even more exciting story of Jesus himself.